# OPHELIA
## the Californian
# Sea Otter

**By Tori Busto**

DORRANCE
PUBLISHING CO
EST. 1920
PITTSBURGH, PENNSYLVANIA 15238

Dorrance Publishing Co
585 Alpha Drive
Suite 103
Pittsburgh, PA 15238
Visit our website at www.dorrancebookstore.com

ISBN: 979-8-8852-7348-0
eISBN: 979-8-8852-7474-6

# OPHELIA
## the Californian
## Sea Otter

By Tori Busto

## Wonder Smiling

Wake up to smiling wonder
Maybe some thunder
Wind blowing
Playmates dancing all day
With raindrops and more thunderstorms
As the light changes softly
To the colors of the night
Come tuck us in
With kisses goodnight
Leave on your
Shining light

Ophelia woke up to a wonderful soft blue sky Saturday morning.
She woke up extra early today full of excitement
on this day in Monterey with a crisp breeze in the air.

Ophelia, Ester and Violet the best of friends
had planned a very special adventure on this Indian summer day.

The light was beginning to change a bit as seasons were changing.
Feather messages in the clouds of pale yellow and blues filled the sky.

The California Sea Otters were swimming north up the coastline
to Point Arena for a fishing fantastic picnic lunch.

Later that evening the Trio had tickets to enjoy an evening
in Stern Grove Park in San Francisco.

The San Francisco Symphony and the San Francisco
Ballet were performing four short stories.
Showtime was scheduled just about twilight that evening.

Somehow on evenings like this nature's magic fills the air.

After Breakfast Ophellia
set off swimmingly over to
Ester and Violets cove
they were twin sisters absolutely
cute as auburn marigolds.
Ophellia, Ester and Violet
have been best
friends since kindergarten.

Ophellia tapped her soft golden sable paw on the door
at the twin sisters nautical front door.

Violet popped out answered the door quickly all dressed up and ready to go.
She was more excited than ever.
Such a lovely day she muttered as she ran off to find Ester.

Ester came out of the back of the cave with a blanket and a picnic basket.
Saying " Hey we need this stuff today my friend ".

Packing up for the day. The Trio set off swimming north as planned to Point Arena.
The fishing was always fantastic near the lighthouse.

With blanket and picnic basket in tow Ophellia, Ester and Violet set off on their magical Saturday. Ophellia was day dreaming the whole time while traveling. Her imagination was busy painting sights and sounds of the evening to come. It was as though she see it and hear it. Tingle shivers her sable otter form so excited.

The Otter Trio set off to swim in the pacific slip stream current the water was moving today swiftly. Lots of Sea Animals out and about.

Seagull's searching above watching the rolling sea waves
for pools of little krill and mackerel fishes.

These fishes were some of Ophellia's snacks as well
as Uni of course is her absolute favorite seafood ever.

Oh and it just so happened that Violet made her special
seaweed salad she is so creative.

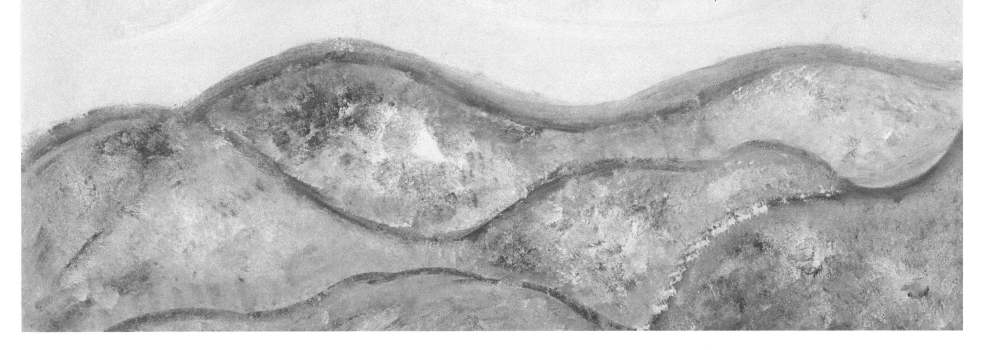

As the ladies approached Point Arena they noticed a group of wild Giraffes
out strolling along the jutted rocks near the shoreline.

Ester pointed to some Mountain Beavers
wondering if they were staying on for the winter season.

Violet's singing something from memory
bopping along having a groovy time la la de de doa doa.

Hummingbirds playing with the flowers and the trees. Nature's voices singing clear for all to hear. Listen to the waves crashing near with sounds around.

It was still early a bit before tea looking at the position of the sun in the late morning sky.

Setting up for fishing Violet found some sea stars and sand dollars what a fortunate find. She decided to collect the starry creatures then placed them carefully back into the waves of the sea.

Fishing along the shoreline Violet came across a seabed of Uni.
Oh how fabulous a find. She called out to Ophellia and Ester
beckoning them to come over to the uni bed.

The trio of Otters only harvested fish for their picnic that evening at the concert.
They made sure to only fish for what they needed
and preserved the crop for their fellow sea animals.

When the hunting and the fishing were completed the otters
packed up the picnic basket. The basket was full of Ophellia's
fabulous seafood salad and Uni from the point Arena Cove.
Plus the girls got lucky the seagulls shared some savory anchovies they had plenty.

GUESS WHAT ???? TIME TO GO!!!!!!!!

Just about then everyone was chillin and swimming around
taking it easy it was time to pack up and swim to San Francisco and Stern Grove.

The light was beginning to change into a silver blue evening sky
light glowing all around. Soft breeze blowing across the waves
as Ophellia, Ester and Violet set off southbound
towards those light that glow so magically in the City by the Bay.

Arriving at the entrance into Stern Grove
the feeling of excitement was in the air.
The symphony was settling in and tuning their instruments.
The Ballet dancers were slipping into
their costumes, shoes and fixing their hair and makeup.

Lots of giggles and silliness everywhere.

Ophellia, Ester and Violet set up the blanket and the picnic baske
under some eucalyptus and redwood trees growing together inside the grove.
The trees are the charm and contribute to the warm crisp sound
that the symphony magically creates whenever they play at this
enchanted place in the city. The sound so warm and wonderful.

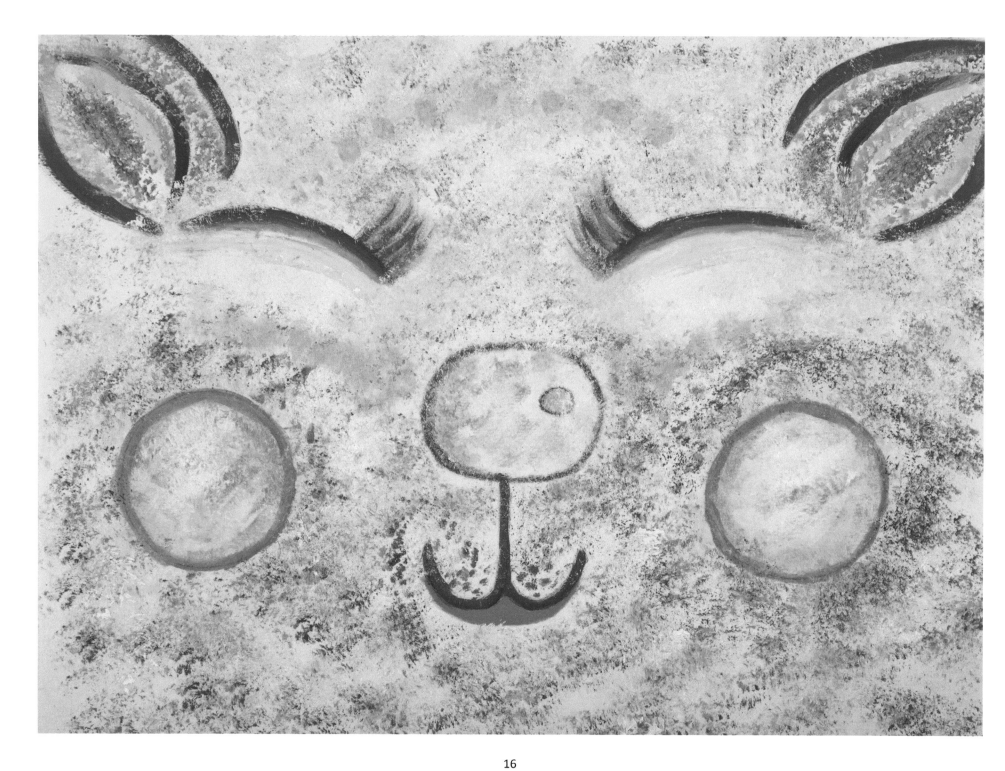

The grove has its own aura or personality.
The eucalyptus and redwood trees stand tall ready to play, sing and dance
with the musicians, dancers and performers. They rehearse and look forward
to the energy that comes alive when everyone gathers together celebrating.
What a treat it is to relax enjoy dancers dancing and performers performing.

Tonight's performance are classical musical and dance works
from Pytor Ilyich Tchaikovsky an absolute fans favorite.

The symphony played with crystal clarity. Some said
the ocean was listening that evening as well.

While enjoying the performance the Trio of Otters
enjoyed sharing their fishing finds from earlier in the day.
The anchovies the seagulls had shared were delicious seriously Unami.

Afterwards Ophellia, Ester and Violet gathered up their belongings.

With their hearts full of happiness the trio of otters
sang and danced all the way home from San Francisco to
their homes in Monterey.

The stars twinkled and sparkled all night long.

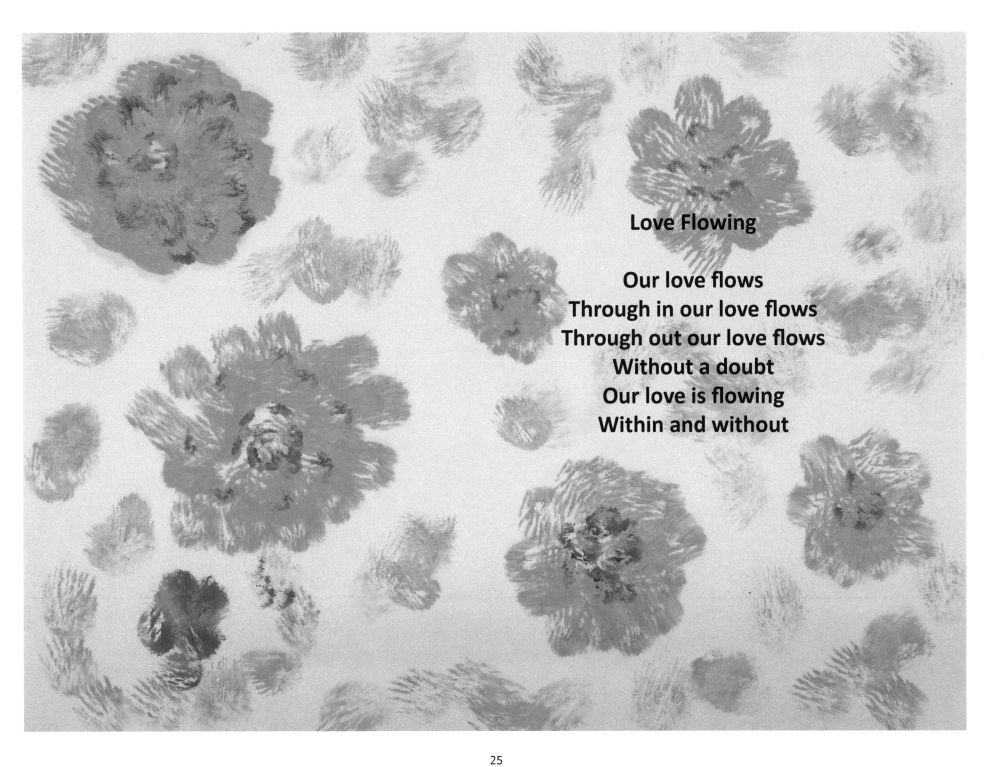

**Love Flowing**

**Our love flows**
**Through in our love flows**
**Through out our love flows**
**Without a doubt**
**Our love is flowing**
**Within and without**